ADORABLE DOGS
COLOUR BY NUMBER

Sachin Sachdeva

This book belongs to

- -

Bassethound

(1) Brown	(2) Red Brown	(3) Lt. Brown
(4) Red	(7) Yellow	(8) Mustard
(9) Lt. Green	(10) Green	(11) Dark Green
(12) Lt. Blue	(13) Sky Blue	(14) Turquoise
(15) Blue	(17) Purple	(19) Magenta
(20) Pink	(21) Peach	(23) Dark Grey
(24) Black		

Border Collie

(1) Brown	(2) Red Brown	(4) Red
(6) Orange	(7) Yellow	(8) Mustard
(9) Lt. Green	(10) Green	(12) Lt. Blue
(13) Sky Blue	(14) Turquoise	(15) Blue
(16) Lavender	(18) Violet	(19) Magenta
(20) Pink	(21) Peach	(22) Grey
(23) Dark Grey	(24) Black	

Setter Dog

(1) Brown	(2) Red Brown	(3) Lt. Brown
(4) Red	(6) Orange	(7) Yellow
(8) Mustard	(10) Green	(11) Dark Green
(12) Lt. Blue	(13) Sky Blue	(15) Blue
(19) Magenta	(20) Pink	(22) Grey
(23) Dark Grey	(24) Black	

Shiba Inu

(1) Brown	(2) Red Brown	(4) Red
(6) Orange	(7) Yellow	(8) Mustard
(10) Green	(11) Dark Green	(12) Lt. Blue
(13) Sky Blue	(14) Turquoise	(15) Blue
(16) Lavender	(19) Magenta	(20) Pink
(22) Grey	(23) Dark Grey	(24) Black

The Great Pyrenees

1) Brown　　2) Red Brown　　3) Lt. Brown

6) Orange　　7) Yellow　　8) Mustard

10) Green　　11) Dark Green　　12) Lt. Blue

13) Sky Blue　　15) Blue　　16) Lavender

19) Magenta　　20) Pink　　21) Peach

22) Grey　　23) Dark Grey　　24) Black

German Shepherd

1 Brown	2 Red Brown	5 Dark Red
6 Orange	7 Yellow	8 Mustard
10 Green	11 Dark Green	12 Lt. Blue
13 Sky Blue	14 Turquoise	15 Blue
16 Lavender	19 Magenta	20 Pink
21 Peach	22 Grey	23 Dark Grey
24 Black		

French Bulldog

1 Brown	2 Red Brown	3 Lt. Brown
4 Red	5 Dark Red	6 Orange
7 Yellow	8 Mustard	10 Green
11 Dark Green	12 Lt. Blue	13 Sky Blue
15 Blue	16 Lavender	17 Purple
18 Violet	20 Pink	22 Grey
23 Dark Grey	24 Black	

Jack Russel Terrier

1 Brown	2 Red Brown	4 Red
5 Dark Red	6 Orange	7 Yellow
8 Mustard	9 Lt. Green	10 Green
11 Dark Green	12 Lt. Blue	13 Sky Blue
14 Turquoise	15 Blue	20 Pink
22 Grey	23 Dark Grey	24 Black

Husky

1) Brown	2) Red Brown	3) Lt. Brown
5) Dark Red	6) Orange	7) Yellow
10) Green	12) Lt. Blue	13) Sky Blue
15) Blue	19) Magenta	20) Pink
22) Grey	23) Dark Grey	24) Black

Bolognese dog

(1) Brown	(2) Red Brown	(4) Red
(6) Orange	(7) Yellow	(8) Mustard
(10) Green	(11) Dark Green	(12) Lt. Blue
(13) Sky Blue	(14) Turquoise	(15) Blue
(16) Lavender	(18) Violet	(19) Magenta
(20) Pink	(21) Peach	(22) Grey
(23) Dark Grey	(24) Black	

Poodle

- (1) Brown
- (2) Red Brown
- (3) Lt. Brown
- (5) Dark Red
- (6) Orange
- (7) Yellow
- (8) Mustard
- (9) Lt. Green
- (10) Green
- (11) Dark Green
- (12) Lt. Blue
- (15) Blue
- (16) Lavender
- (17) Purple
- (18) Violet
- (19) Magenta
- (20) Pink
- (21) Peach
- (22) Grey
- (23) Dark Grey
- (24) Black

Dalmatian

(2) Red Brown	(3) Lt. Brown	(6) Orange
(7) Yellow	(8) Mustard	(10) Green
(11) Dark Green	(12) Lt. Blue	(15) Blue
(16) Lavender	(17) Purple	(18) Violet
(20) Pink	(21) Peach	(22) Grey
(23) Dark Grey	(24) Black	

Papillon

1 Brown	2 Red Brown	4 Red
6 Orange	8 Mustard	10 Green
12 Lt. Blue	15 Blue	16 Lavender
19 Magenta	20 Pink	21 Peach
24 Black		

Labrador

① Brown	② Red Brown	⑤ Dark Red
⑥ Orange	⑦ Yellow	⑧ Mustard
⑨ Lt. Green	⑩ Green	⑪ Dark Green
⑫ Lt. Blue	⑬ Sky Blue	⑮ Blue
⑳ Pink	㉓ Dark Grey	㉔ Black

Afghan Hound

1 Brown	2 Red Brown	4 Red
5 Dark Red	6 Orange	7 Yellow
10 Green	11 Dark Green	12 Lt. Blue
14 Turquoise	15 Blue	16 Lavender
21 Peach	22 Grey	23 Dark Grey
24 Black		

Komondor

1 Brown	2 Red Brown	4 Red
7 Yellow	10 Green	11 Dark Green
12 Lt. Blue	13 Sky Blue	15 Blue
16 Lavender	18 Violet	19 Magenta
20 Pink	21 Peach	22 Grey
23 Dark Grey	24 Black	

South Russian Shepherd

1) Brown
2) Red Brown
3) Lt. Brown

4) Red
5) Dark Red
6) Orange

10) Green
11) Dark Green
12) Lt. Blue

15) Blue
20) Pink
21) Peach

22) Grey
23) Dark Grey
24) Black

Chinese Crested

(1) Brown	(2) Red Brown	(4) Red
(5) Dark Red	(6) Orange	(7) Yellow
(8) Mustard	(10) Green	(11) Dark Green
(12) Lt. Blue	(15) Blue	(17) Purple
(19) Magenta	(20) Pink	(21) Peach
(23) Dark Grey	(24) Black	

Pomeranian

1) Brown	2) Red Brown	5) Dark Red
6) Orange	7) Yellow	8) Mustard
10) Green	11) Dark Green	12) Lt. Blue
19) Magenta	20) Pink	21) Peach
24) Black		

Shih Tzu

2 Red Brown 4 Red 5 Dark Red

6 Orange 7 Yellow 8 Mustard

10 Green 11 Dark Green 12 Lt. Blue

13 Sky Blue 15 Blue 18 Violet

19 Magenta 20 Pink 21 Peach

22 Grey 23 Dark Grey 24 Black

Bichon Frise

3 Lt. Brown   4 Red   6 Orange

7 Yellow   8 Mustard   12 Lt. Blue

14 Turquoise   15 Blue   23 Dark Grey

24 Black

NewFoundland

(1) Brown	(2) Red Brown	(3) Lt. Brown
(4) Red	(5) Dark Red	(6) Orange
(7) Yellow	(8) Mustard	(12) Lt. Blue
(14) Turquoise	(15) Blue	(16) Lavender
(17) Purple	(19) Magenta	(20) Pink
(22) Grey	(23) Dark Grey	(24) Black

Tibetan Mastiff

1) Brown	2) Red Brown	3) Lt. Brown
4) Red	6) Orange	7) Yellow
8) Mustard	9) Lt. Green	10) Green
11) Dark Green	12) Lt. Blue	13) Sky Blue
15) Blue	16) Lavender	18) Violet
19) Magenta	20) Pink	22) Grey
23) Dark Grey	24) Black	

Kintamani

1) Brown   2) Red Brown   4) Red

6) Orange   7) Yellow   8) Mustard

9) Lt. Green 10) Green   11) Dark Green

12) Lt. Blue 13) Sky Blue   15) Blue

16) Lavender 17) Purple   18) Violet

19) Magenta   20) Pink   21) Peach

22) Grey   23) Dark Grey   24) Black

Pompom

1. Brown
2. Red Brown
6. Orange
7. Yellow
8. Mustard
10. Green
11. Dark Green
14. Turquoise
15. Blue
17. Purple
19. Magenta
20. Pink
21. Peach
22. Grey
23. Dark Grey
24. Black

YOUR FEEDBACK MATTERS

The coloring community has been very supportive to us and I further request you to leave a review on our books.

By leaving a review, you're supporting an independent artist and author you buy from and shares your unique experience with future buyers.

Thank you,
Sachin Sachdeva
(Artist & Author)

SAY HELLO!!

I receive lots of email from colourist all around the world and it really feels good to see how much love you're pouring in towards our books by sharing your coloured pages with us. Thank you so much.

If there's any feedback or suggestions, please write to me. I respond to all the emails :-)

Email - sachin@sachinsachdev.com
Page - facebook.com/sachdevbooks
Group - facebook.com/groups/sachinsachdevabooks
Books - amazon.com/author/sachinsachdeva
Instagram - @sachdev.art (#sachinsachdeva)

Color by Number & Non-CBN for Adults

1	Magical Artifacts CBN	☑
2	Beautiful Birds CBN & Non-CBN	☐
3	Flowers & Butterflies CBN	☐
4	Doll House CBN & Non-CBN	☐
5	Power Quotes CBN	☐
6	Paisley Designs CBN	☐
7	Spring Season CBN & Non-CBN	☐
8	50 Bible Verses CBN	☐
9	50 Gorgeous Patterns CBN & Non-CBN	☐
10	50 Tribal Masks CBN & Non-CBN	☐
11	50 Arabic Patterns CBN & Non-CBN (2023 release)	☐
12	50 Psalm Quotes CBN & Non-CBN (2023 release)	☐
13	Christmas in July CBN & Non-CBN (2023 release)	☐
14	50 Dreamcatchers CBN & Non-CBN (2023 release)	☐

Mosaic Art - Color by Number for Adults

1	Sea Creatures - 5x5 mm	☐
2	Inside Home - 5x5 mm	☐
3	Vintage Cars - 3x3 mm	☐
4	Patterns - 3x3 mm	☐
5	Vacations - 3x3 mm	☐
6	Musical - 3x3 mm	☐
7	Christmas - 3x3 mm	☐
8	Exotic Birds - 3x3 mm	☐
9	Wild Flowers - 3x3 mm	☐
10	Xmas Patterns - 3x3 mm	☐
11	100 Easy Designs - 7x7 mm (2023 release)	☐
12	Landscapes - 3x3 mm (2023 release)	☐
13	Halloween - 3x3 mm (2023 release)	☐

Stained Glass - Color by Number & Non-CBN

1	Nautical Designs CDN & Non-CBN	☐
2	Tiffany Windows CBN & Non-CBN	☐
3	Egyptian Designs CBN & Non-CBN	☐
4	Halloween CBN & Non-CBN	☐
5	Christmas CBN & Non-CBN	☐
6	Wildlife CBN & Non-CBN	☐
7	Sugar Skulls CBN & Non-CBN	☐
8	Valentine CBN & Non-CBN (2023 release)	☐
9	Joyful Nature CBN & Non-CBN (2023 release)	☐
10	Countryside Scenes CBN & Non-CBN (2023 release)	☐

Mandalas - Color by Number & Non-CBN

1	Mandalas - Adult Coloring Book	☐
2	Christmas Mandalas CBN	☐
3	50 Animal Mandalas CBN & Non-CBN	☐
4	50 Diamond Mandalas CBN & Non-CBN	☐
5	50 Halloween Mandalas CBN & Non-CBN	☐
6	50 Christmas Mandalas CBN & Non-CBN	☐
7	50 Celestial Mandalas CBN & Non-CBN	☐
8	100 Easy Mandalas CBN & Non-CBN (Vol 1)	☐
9	50 Autumn Mandalas CBN & Non-CBN	☐
10	50 Winter Mandalas CBN & Non-CBN	☐
11	50 Steampunk Mandalas CBN & Non-CBN (2023 release)	☐

Chibi Coloring Books (CBN & Non-CBN)

1	Chibi Halloween and spooky characters (2023 release)	☐
2	**Chibi Girls and adorable pets (coming soon)**	

Coloring Book for Adults

1	I am Capable of Amazing Things	☐
2	Nail Art - A Fun Coloring Book for Girls	☐
3	Ramadan Mubarak - Adult Coloring Book	☐
4	Spring Season - The Coloring Book for Adults	☐
5	Butterflies Coloring Book	☐
6	Christmas - The Adult Coloring Book	☐
7	Sugar Skulls - The Adult Coloring Book	☐
8	Flowers Bloom - Coloring Book for Adults	☐

Color by Number Books

#	Title		#	Title	
1	Sea Life	☐	23	Love Treats	☐
2	Cute Cats	☐	24	Dress Up	☐
3	Cute Dinosaurs	☐	25	Cute Llamas	☐
4	Pirates	☐	26	Cute Sloths	☐
5	Butterfly	☐	27	100 Large Print	☐
6	Mermaid	☐	28	Christmas Advent Calendar	☐
7	Easter	☐	29	Funny Food Monsters (2023 release)	☐
8	Flowers & Butterflies	☐	30	Playful Crocodile (2023 release)	☐
9	Christmas	☐	31	Adorable Dogs (2023 release)	☐
10	Festive Christmas - 50 Pages	☐	32	**Mythical Creatures (coming soon)**	
11	Happy Halloween	☐			
12	Trick or Treat	☐			
13	Halloween	☐			
14	Cute Animals	☐			
15	St. Patrick's Day	☐			
16	Vehicles	☐			
17	A day at the Circus	☐			
18	Sugar Skulls	☐			
19	Cakes & Candies	☐			
20	Birds	☐			
21	Mandala	☐			
22	Magical	☐			

Mystery Circles - Color by Number

1	Happy Easter CBN	
2	Happy Halloween CBN	
3	Happy Christmas CBN	
4	Happy Spring CBN (2023 release)	

Best Selling Collection Books

1	The Greatest Hits of Sachin Sachdeva - 100 Color by Number	
2	All Time Hits - 100 Color by Number	
3	Best Collection - 100 Coloring Pages	
4	Stained Glass Collection - 50 Color by Number	
5	Doodle n Color Collection - 100 Pages CBN & Non-CBN (2023 release)	
6	**Magnificent Mandalas Collection - 100 Color by Number (coming soon)**	

Papercut Art - Color by Number

1	Halloween CBN	
2	Advent Calendar - Christmas (CBN, Non-CBN, CBC)	
3	Little Dwarfs (CBN, Non-CBN, CBC)	
4	Silhouettes CBN (Black Lines Edition)	

Doodle n Color Coloring Books

1	Paisley Patterns	
2	Day of the Dead	
3	Flowers & Butterflies	
4	Dazzling Fashion Art	
5	Cakes & Candies	
6	Be Mine Valentine	
7	Mandala Designs	
8	Magical & Mystic Art	

Color Chart Sheet

Medium: _____   Brand: _____

_____

_____

_____

_____

_____

_____

_____

_____

_____

_____

_____

Color Chart Sheet

Medium: _____

Brand: _____

_____

_____

_____

_____

_____

_____

_____

_____

_____

_____

_____

Color Chart Sheet

Medium: _____   Brand: _____

_____   _____

_____   _____

_____   _____

_____   _____

_____   _____

_____   _____

_____   _____

_____   _____

_____   _____

_____   _____

_____   _____

_____   _____

Color Chart Sheet

Medium: _____   Brand: _____

Color Testing Sheet

Made in the USA
Middletown, DE
04 October 2023

40127971R00040